Snow Place like Home!

the Incredible Snowkids of marshmallow mountain

Snow Place Like Home!

Editorial Director: Todd Hafer
Editors: Theresa Trinder & Megan Langford
Art Director: Kevin Swanson
Designer: Michelle Nicole Nicolier
Production Artist: Dan C. Horton

Printed and bound in China.
ISBN: 978-1-59530-131-4
1LPR7501

The snowkids of Marshmallow Mountain were meeting

one troublesome Tuesday at two.

They all gathered round in their clubhouse,

Fort Snowpack, to try to decide what to do.

Then Snow-Joe (their president) rose to his feet.
"My Dad says this place used to rock!
There were tourists and festivals all through the year,
and stuff going on round the clock!

"'Cause Marshmallow Mountain was known as the home
of the world's most incredible candy. . ."

"So THAT'S what they made in that empty old factory
on Candy Cane Lane!" added Andy.

"Hey, let's check it out!" said the twins, Fridge and Midge,
and all of the snowkids agreed.
They started out walking . . . all except Spike,
who snowboarded there at top speed!

Snow-Joe explained as they wandered inside,

"That's the Candy Contraption, you know!

The famous machine that made all kinds of treats . . .

but I guess it broke down years ago."

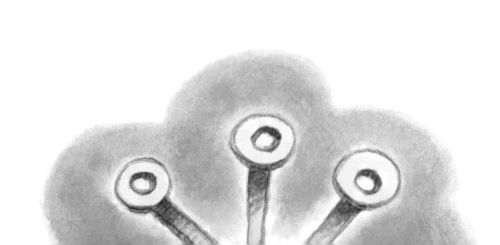

"I bet I could find some spare parts for that thing,"
said Spike, whose ideas were great.
He knew all the junkyards that had the best stuff
for the sculptures he liked to create.

"And I'll find the recipes!" Freeze Louise offered.
"I bet they've been all tucked away
in grandmothers' cookbooks and family kitchens.
I better start looking today!"

Fridge and Midge painted some colorful flyers
their fine feathered friends could deliver.
Snow-Joe and Andy sped off on their skates
to tell all the snowfolk downriver.

Soon everyone heard what the snowkids were doing.

"I tell you, those kids have got spunk!"

"There hasn't been this much excitement in town
since the Candy Contraption went CLUNK!"

Then Snow-Joe announced it was time for a test.
Each pulley and gear was in place,
each special ingredient poured in the hopper,
a huge, hopeful smile on each face.

The wheels started whirring! The spoons started stirring!

And out popped one peppermint kiss.

They waited . . . and waited . . . 'til Freeze Louise shouted,

"It's GOT to go faster than THIS!"

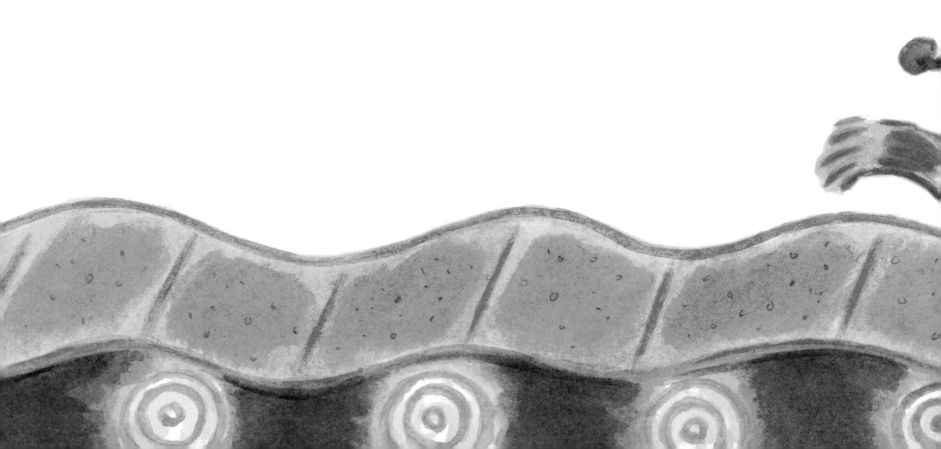

Then Andy's quick brain made some quick calculations
and soon he'd adjusted each dial.
Then candy came rocketing out by the dozens,
creating a mountainous pile!

The snowkids got busy with boxing and bagging

(and tasting a sample or two).

They labeled and loaded and made their deliveries,

and each had a fun job to do!

The news got around that the snowkids had done it!
They'd gotten things rolling again!
And Marshmallow Mountain was just as exciting
as snowfolk remembered "back when."

From Shiverdale Corners to Snowberry Falls,

Chill Valley to Icicle Run,

they came for a taste of that world-famous candy . . .

and stayed for the warm, friendly fun.

We'd love to hear from you
if you have enjoyed this book.

PLEASE SEND YOUR COMMENTS TO:
Book Feedback, Mail Drop 215
2501 McGee, Kansas City, MO 64108

OR EMAIL US AT:
booknotes@hallmark.com